W9-CTO-680

ANIMAL STORIES
for
Children

By
Rajesh Kavassery

YOUNG KIDS PRESS
An imprint of Sura Books (Pvt) Ltd.

(An ISO 9001: 2000 Certified Company)

Chennai ● Ernakulam ● Bengalooru

Price: Rs.50.00

© PUBLISHERS

ANIMAL STORIES FOR CHILDREN

by Rajesh Kavassery

This Edition : August, 2008

Size : 1/8 Crown

Pages : 128

Price: Rs.50.00

ISBN : 81-7478-863-8

YOUNG KIDS PRESS

[An imprint of Sura Books (Pvt) Ltd.]

Head Office: 1620, 'J' Block, 16th Main Road, Anna Nagar, **Chennai - 600 040.**
Phones: 044-26162173, 26161099

Branches :
- XXXII/2328, New Kalavath Road, Opp. to BSNL, Near Chennoth Glass, Palarivattom, **Ernakulam - 682 025.** Phone: 0484-3205797, 2535636
- 3638/A, IVth Cross, Opp. to Malleswaram Railway Station, Gayathri Nagar, Back gate of Subramaniya Nagar, **Bengalooru - 560 021.** Phone: 080-23324950

Printed at T.Krishna Press, Chennai - 600 102 and Published by V.V.K.Subburaj for Young Kids Press [An imprint of Sura Books (Pvt) Ltd.] 1620, 'J' Block, 16th Main Road, Anna Nagar, Chennai - 600 040. Phones: 91-44-26162173, 26161099. Fax: (91) 44-26162173. e-mail: enquiry@surabooks.com, website: www.surabooks.com

08 08 2000

CONTENTS

		PAGE
1.	THE RABBIT AND THE FOX	1
2.	THE CLEVER FOX	3
3.	THE TWO OXEN AND THE GOAT	5
4.	THE FOUR NEIGHBOURS	7
5.	THE FOOLISH DOVES	9
6.	THE FOOLISH MONKEYS	12
7.	THE CLEVER TURTLE AND THE FOOLISH KING	14
8.	THE WISE DEER AND THE WICKED FOXES	17
9.	THE CROOKED RAT	20
10.	THE INTELLIGENT DEER	22
11.	THE TIGER AND THE FOX	25
12.	THE MAGICIAN AND THE TIGER	28
13.	THE FOOLHARDY WOLF	31
14.	THE DONKEY AND THE DOG	34
15.	THE TIGER AND THE DOVE	36
16.	THE FOX AND THE OTTERS	38
17.	THE CAMEL'S CLEVERNESS	41
18.	THE THREE FISHES	43
19.	THE KNOWLEDGEABLE FOX	45
20.	THE TRICKY FOX AND THE RATS	47
21.	THE TIGER AND THE FOX	50
22.	THE FOOLISH BIRDS	52

23. THE LION AND THE DEER 54

24. THE STUPID YOUNG RABBIT 57

25. THE HUMBLE SWAN AND THE BOASTFUL CROW 59

26. CHARLIE FOX AND THE ROOSTER 61

27. THE HALF-EDUCATED JACKAL 64

28. THE CROOKED TOWN MOUSE 68

29. THE DOG AND THE DOLPHIN 71

30. THE TORTOISE AND THE BIRDS 73

31. THE RABBIT'S MOTHER 77

32. THE CLEVER LAMB 82

33. THE DEER AND THE FARMER 84

34. THE CUNNING ROOSTERS 89

35. THE FOOLISH LION 92

36. THE STUPID DOG 95

37. THE PEACEMAKERS 97

38. THE LION AND THE CRANE 100

39. WHY THE BEAR HAS A SHORT TAIL? 102

40. THE COUNTRY MOUSE AND THE TOWN MOUSE 104

41. THE DIRTY DEER 107

42. TIGER GOES ABROAD 110

43. THE FOOLISH LEOPARD 112

44. THE CLEVER SPARROW 117

45. THE CAT AND THE RAT 120

Animal Stories for Children

1. THE RABBIT AND THE FOX

Once upon a time, there lived a crooked fox who, one day got some tar and made a Tar Baby. He brought a hat from his den, put it on the head of that Tar Baby and kept it in the middle of the road. Then, to see what would happen, he hid behind a bush.

After some time, a rabbit came there. He politely wished the Tar Baby 'Good Morning'. When it did not respond he wished it again and then yet again. Finally, thinking the Tar Baby was being deliberately rude, he punched on its chest and of course, his hand got stuck in the tar. He punched it with the other hand and that hand too got stuck. When he tried kicking it, his legs got stuck.

The fox came out of his hiding place and rolled on the ground with laughter.

Then he said to the rabbit, "O Rabbit! I will roast you for my dinner."

"O Fox! You can roast me if you want," said the rabbit, "but please don't throw me into that briar patch."

"I'll hang you before roasting you," said the fox.

"Do that," said the rabbit, "but for heaven's sake, don't throw me into that briar patch."

"I'll drown you," said the fox. But, the rabbit didn't seem afraid of that either.

"You can kill me in any way, but don't throw me into that briar patch," he begged.

This made the fox think that the briar patch was a dangerous place for the rabbit. Then he immediately plucked out the rabbit from the Tar Baby, and flung him into the patch of thorny bushes.

He waited expectantly for the cry of pain, but heard nothing. Instead, after some time he saw the rabbit sitting cross-legged way up on a nearby hill, and grinning at him.

"I was born and bred in a briar patch, O Foolish Fox!" the rabbit shouted.

2. THE CLEVER FOX

One day, the king of animals, the lion called all his subjects to his abode, a vast, smelly cave.

The monkey felt nauseated by the smell and held his nose. The lion was offended by this act of the monkey and gave him a huge blow that knocked him senseless.

"Does my cave smell bad?" he asked the bear.

"Not at all, Your Highness," said the bear, ingratiatingly. "I would say your cave smells like a bouquet of flowers."

The lion knew this was not possible and knocked him senseless too.

The other animals, including a fox, began to sidle out of the cave, but the lion caught the fox's tail and pulled him back.

"Let us have your opinion too," he said. "Does my cave smell bad?"

"I have a terrible cold, Your Highness," said the fox cunningly, forcing a sneeze. "I cannot smell anything now. So, I cannot tell you whether your cave smells bad or not."

The lion liked his clever reply and made him his minister.

3. THE TWO OXEN AND THE GOAT

Once upon a time, there was an ox named Big Black. He had a younger brother named Little Black. These two brothers did all the carting on a large farm.

Now the farmer had an only daughter and she was soon to be married. Her mother gave orders that the goat should be fattened for the wedding feast.

Little Black noticed that the goat was fed on choice food. He said to his brother, "How is it, Big Black, that you and I are given only straw and grass to eat, while we do all the hard work on the farm? That lazy goat does nothing, but eat the choice food the farmer gives him."

His brother said, "My dear Little Black, envy him not. That lazy goat is eating the food of death! He is being fattened for the wedding feast. Eat your straw and grass and be content and live long."

Not long afterwards, the fattened goat was killed and cooked for the wedding feast.

Then Big Black said, "Did you see, Little Black, what became of the goat after all his fine feeding?"

"Yes," said the little brother, "we can go on eating plain food for years, but the poor goat ate the food of death and now he is dead. His feed was good while it lasted, but it did not last long."

4. THE FOUR NEIGHBOURS

Once upon a time, there lived four animals, a wild cat, a mongoose, a mouse and an owl, who had made their home in a huge banyan tree.

The mouse and the mongoose lived at the foot of the tree in two different holes. The cat lived in a large hole halfway up the tree and the owl lived in the branches.

The cat was not afraid of its neighbours and moved about fearlessly. The owl and the mongoose were afraid of the cat and kept a safe distance from it. The mouse lived in mortal dread of all its three neighbours.

One day, the cat was caught in a net laid by a hunter. Its three neighbours watched with glee as it struggled to get out of the net in which it had been ensnared.

They knew it was a hopeless task. Soon the hunter would come and they would be rid of their enemy forever. The rat's joy, however, was shortlived because even as it watched the cat struggle, it became aware that the mongoose was moving menacingly towards it. Looking up, it saw that the owl too was getting ready to swoop down. The rat realised that it was in grave danger and that the only one who could save it was its arch-enemy, the cat.

It leaped on the net in which the cat was caught and began nibbling at it. Within a short time it had made a hole big enough for the cat to squeeze through. Seeing the cat come out, the owl and the mongoose fled.

The rat too ran away. It knew it could not expect any gratitude from the cat, but in saving it, it had saved its own life.

❋ ❋ ❋

5. THE FOOLISH DOVES

Once upon a time, many doves lived together in a forest. The wisest of them all was their leader.

A man lived near the forest and earned his living by catching doves and selling them. Day after day he listened to the note of the leader calling the doves. By and by this

man, the fowler, was able to call the doves together. Hearing the note, the doves thought it was their leader that called.

When they were crowded together, the fowler threw his net over them and off he went into the town, where he soon sold all the doves that he had caught.

The wise leader saw the plan of the fowler for catching the doves. He called the birds to him and said, "This fowler is carrying away so many of us. So, we must put a stop to it. I have thought of a plan; it is this: The next time the fowler throws a net over you, each of you must put your head through one of the little holes in the net. Then all of you together must fly away to the nearest thorn-bush. You can leave the net on the thorn-bush and be free yourselves."

The doves said that, that was a very good plan and they would try it the next time the fowler threw the net over them.

The very next day the fowler came and called them together. Then he threw the net over them. The doves lifted the net and flew away with it to the nearest thorn-bush where they left it. Then they flew back to their leader to tell him how well his plan had worked.

The fowler was busy until evening getting his net off the thorns and he went home empty-handed. The next day the same thing happened, and the next. His wife was angry because he did not bring home any money, but the fowler said, "The fact is those doves are working together now. The moment my net is over them, off they fly with it, leaving it on a thorn-bush. As soon as the doves begin to quarrel I shall be able to catch them."

Not long after this, one of the doves in alighting on their feeding ground, trod by accident on another's head. "Who trod on my head?" angrily cried the second. "I did; but I didn't mean to. Don't be angry," said the first dove, but the second dove was angry and said mean things.

Soon all the doves had taken sides in this quarrel. When the fowler came that day he flung his net over them, and this time instead of flying off with it, one side said, "Now, you lift the net," and the other side said, "Lift it yourself."

"You try to make us lift it all," said the doves on one side. "No, we won't!" said the others, "you begin and we will help." But, neither side began.

So the doves quarrelled, and while they were quarrelling, the fowler caught them all in his net. He took them to town and sold them for a good price.

6. THE FOOLISH MONKEYS

Once upon a time, there lived a monkey-trainer who was fond of monkeys. He kept several of them in his house. He understood their language and they understood his.

Once when the province was stricken by drought and food was scarce, he decided to reduce their daily ration of bananas.

The master told the monkeys, "From tomorrow, I'll give you three bananas in the morning and four in the evening. You will have to be satisfied with that."

The monkeys were very angry on hearing this and created an uproar with their chattering.

"All right, all right," said the master, after a while.

"No need to get so upset. I'll give you four bananas in the morning and three in the evening."

The foolish monkeys were satisfied and immediately quietened down.

❀ ❀ ❀

7. THE CLEVER TURTLE AND THE FOOLISH KING

Once a King had a lake made in the courtyard for the young princes to play in. They swam about in it, and sailed their boats and rafts on it. One day, the King told them that he had asked the men to put some fishes into the lake.

Immediately the boys ran off to see the fishes. Now, along with the fishes, there was a turtle. The boys were delighted with the fishes, but they had never seen a turtle, and they were afraid of it, thinking it was a demon. They

ran back to their father, crying, "There is a demon on the bank of the lake."

The King ordered his men to catch the demon, and bring it to the palace. When the turtle was brought in, the boys cried and ran away.

The King was very fond of his sons, so he ordered the men who had brought the turtle to kill it.

"How shall we kill it?" they asked.

"Pound it to powder," said someone. "Bake it in hot coals," said another.

So one plan after another was spoken of. Then an old man who had always been afraid of the water said, "Throw the thing into the lake where it flows out over the rocks into the river. Then it will surely be killed."

When the turtle heard what the old man said, he thrust out his head and asked, "Friend, what have I done that you should do such a dreadful thing as that to me? The other plans were bad enough, but to throw me into the lake! Don't speak of such a cruel thing!"

When the King heard what the turtle said, he told his men to take the turtle at once and throw it into the lake.

The turtle laughed to himself as he slid away down the river to his old home.

"Good!" he said, "those people do not know how safe I am in the water!"

8. THE WISE DEER AND THE WICKED FOXES

Once upon a time, many, many wild deer lived in a cave in the side of a hill. A fox lived with his mate not far from this cave. Like all the foxes they liked the taste of deer-meat. So they caught deer, one after another, and ate them all but the one who was wiser than all the others. Try as they might, the foxes could not catch her.

One day, the fox said to his mate, "My dear, let us play a trick on that wise deer. I will lie down here pretending to be dead. You go alone to the cave where the deer lives, and looking very sad, say to her: 'My dear, do you see my mate lying there dead? I am so sad; I have no friends. Will you be good to me? Will you come and help me bury the body of my mate?' The deer will be sorry for you and I think she will come here with you. When she stands beside me I will spring upon her and bite her in the neck. Then she will fall over dead, and we shall have good meat to eat."

The fox then lay down, and his mate went to the deer, saying what she had been told to say.

But, the wise deer said, "My dear, all my family and friends have been eaten by your mate. I am afraid to go even one step with you. I am far safer here than I would be there."

"Do not be afraid," said the fox. "What harm can a dead fox do to you?"

These and many more words the fox said to the deer, so that at last the deer said she would go with the fox.

But, as they went up the hill side by side, the deer said to herself, "Who knows what will happen? How do I know the fox is dead?"

Then she said to the fox, "I think it will be better if you go on in front of me."

The fox thought he heard them coming. He was hungry and he raised up his head to see if he could see them. The deer saw him raise his head, and she turned and ran back to her cave.

"Why did you raise your head when you were pretending to be dead?" the fox asked her mate. He had no good answer.

By and by, both the foxes were very hungry that the fox asked his mate to try once more to catch the deer.

This time the fox went to the deer and said, "My friend, your coming helped us, for as soon as you came, my mate felt better. He is now very much better. Come and talk to him. Let us be friends and have a good time together."

The wise deer thought, "These wicked foxes want to play another trick on me. But, I have thought of a trick to play on them." So the deer said, "I will come to see your mate, and I will take my friends with me. You go back and get ready for us. Let us all have a good time together."

Then the fox was afraid, and she asked, "Who are the friends who will come with you? Tell me their names."

The wise deer said, "I will bring the two hounds, Old Gray and Young Tan, and that big dog called Tiger. And I will ask each of them to bring his mate."

The fox waited to hear no more. She turned, and immediately ran back to her mate. The deer never saw either of them again.

9. THE CROOKED RAT

Once upon a time, there lived a crooked rat. One day, when he was about to emerge from his hole, he espied a cat outside. He went back to the colony of rats at the bottom of the hole and invited one of his acquaintances to join him in a visit to a nearby cornfield.

"I would've gone alone," he said, "but I could not deny myself the pleasure of your distinguished company."

"I'll certainly come," said the acquaintance, pleased. "Lead on."

"Lead!" exclaimed the other. "How could I walk in front of a rat as great and illustrious as you? It is you who must lead and I'll follow!"

Greatly flattered, the acquaintance led the way out of the hole and was promptly caught by the cat.

The crooked rat slipped out unnoticed and went on his way.

10. THE INTELLIGENT DEER

Dancil, an intelligent deer, was known for his cleverness. Several times he had fooled the big, bad crocodile, Croco.

Dancil's home was full of trees and food. So, Dancil had no trouble in finding food when he was hungry. Dancil spent his days running and jumping, and his favourite pastime was to look at his own reflection in the river.

Croco and a few other crocodiles lived in the river and were waiting for a chance to have Dancil for dinner.

One day, as Dancil was walking by the riverside, he saw red and ripe fruits hanging on the trees across the river. Dancil wanted to taste the delicious looking fruits because he was getting tired of eating only leaves on his side of the river. He walked to the riverbank and thought hard how to cross the river with Croco waiting for him at the bottom of the river.

Dancil thought and thought and suddenly an idea came to him. He called out to Croco, "Croco! Croco!"

Slowly Croco emerged from the water.

"What is it, Dancil? Why are you shouting my name? Aren't you afraid that I would grab you and have you for dinner?" asked Croco, opening his big mouth.

"Of course, I am afraid, but I have a mission to do. The King has ordered me to count the crocodiles in the river. He is having a feast and all of you are invited to attend. There will be plenty of food, but first I need to count how many of you are here. So, would you please ask your fellow crocodiles to line up across the river so that I can count you up?" said Dancil.

Croco was excited. He gathered all the crocodiles in the river and told them about the feast. Soon all the crocodiles made a line across the river.

"Don't try to eat me while I am counting. Otherwise I would not be able to report to the King," warned Dancil.

"We won't eat you," the crocodiles promised.

Dancil stepped on top of Croco's head and counted one. When he came to the second crocodile, Dancil counted two and so to the rest of the line until he reached the other side of the river.

Dancil turned to Croco and said, "Thank you, Croco for helping me to cross the river. This is my new home."

"What do you mean? You tricked us to help you cross the river?" shouted Croco. He was shocked. "There isn't any feast, is there?" The other crocodiles looked at Croco angrily. They knew they had been tricked.

After that, Dancil lived happily in his new home and had plenty of tasty fruits and green leaves to eat. Croco, however, was ignored by the other crocodiles because of his foolishness.

11. THE TIGER AND THE FOX

One day, a young tiger came suddenly upon a fox. The fox was not able to get away, so he said to the tiger, "Please, Great Tiger, could you take me to your den, and let me live with you and your mate? I will work for you all my days."

This young tiger had been told by his father and mother not to make friends with any fox. But, when this fox called him 'Great Tiger', he said to himself, "This fox is not bad. This fox is not like other foxes." So he took the fox to the den where he lived with his father and mother.

Now this tiger's father was a fine old tiger, and he told his son that he did not like having that fox there. But, the young tiger thought he knew better than his father. So, the fox stayed on in the den.

One day, the fox wanted horse-flesh to eat. So, he said to the young tiger, "Sir, there is nothing we have not eaten, except horse-meat; let us take a horse."

"But, where can we get a horse?" asked the tiger.

"There are small ponies on the river bank," said the fox.

So the young tiger went with the fox to the river bank where the ponies were bathing. The tiger caught a small pony, and throwing it on his back, he ran back to his den.

His father said, "My son, those ponies belong to the King. Kings have many skilful archers. Those tigers do not live long who eat ponies belonging to the King. Do not take another pony."

But, the young tiger liked the taste of horse-meat, and he caught and killed pony after pony.

Soon the King heard that a tiger was killing the ponies when they went to bathe in the river. "Build a tank inside the town," said the King. "The tiger will not get the ponies there." But, the tiger killed the ponies as they bathed in the tank too.

Then the King said that the ponies must be kept in the stables. But, the tiger went over the wall, and killed the ponies in their stables.

At last the King called an archer, who shot like lightning. "Do you think you can shoot this tiger?" the King asked him. The archer said that he was sure he could. "Very well," said the King, "take your place in the tower on the wall, and shoot him." So the archer waited there in the tower.

By and by the tiger and the fox came to the wall. The fox did not go over the wall, but waited to see what would happen. The tiger sprang over the wall. Very soon he caught and killed a pony. Then the archer let fly an arrow.

The tiger roared, "I am shot."

Then the fox said to himself, "The tiger has been shot, and soon he will die. I will now go back to my old home in the woods." And so he did.

The foolish tiger met his end.

12. THE MAGICIAN AND THE TIGER

Once upon a time, there lived a magician. One day, when he was demonstrating his tricks, he took out a rabbit from his hat. The amused spectators applauded the magician.

Unknown to the magician and the spectators, there was a tiger watching the show from behind some bushes, nearby. Later that night, the tiger waylaid the magician as he was going home.

"I saw you pull a rabbit out of your hat," the tiger said. "Now you pull out a cub for me!"

"The rabbit was in the bag all the time," blurted the magician, trembling from head to toe. "I cannot create animals out of thin air!"

"Produce a tiger cub if you know what's good for you!" snarled the tiger.

"All right, all right!" said the magician, thinking fast. "But, it'll take some time. A month at least."

"I can wait!" said the tiger.

"There's another thing," said the magician, a plan forming in his mind. "You'll have to stay on a diet of milk and rice during the entire period!"

"Milk and rice!"

"Otherwise the trick will not work."

"All right," said the tiger, finally. "I'll live on milk and rice."

He went away and returned a month later.

"Now let me have the cub," he said, in a barely audible voice, his diet having made him extremely weak.

The magician called the whole village to witness the magic trick.

"This is a special show for our guest here," he announced. "So instead of pulling out a rabbit from my hat I'll pull out a young member of his family."

He muttered some mumbo-jumbo, passed his hands over the hat several times, and then with a loud cry plunged his hand into the hat and pulled out a small cuddly animal.

"A kitten!" guffawed the spectators.

The kitten meowed.

The tiger was not amused. He let out a mighty roar,

but in his weakened state, the sound that emerged from his mouth was a loud, "Meeeee-Ooowww!"

The villagers rocked with laughter. The tiger felt so ashamed that he leapt out of his seat and ran away.

13. THE FOOLHARDY WOLF

A tiger bounded forth from his lair one day, looking north, west, south and east. He saw a buffalo and went to kill him.

The tiger ate all of the buffalo-meat he wanted, and then went down to the lake for a drink.

As the tiger turned to go toward his den for a nap, he came upon a hungry wolf.

The wolf had no chance to get away, so he threw himself at the tiger's feet.

"What do you want?" the tiger asked.

"O Tiger! Let me be your servant," said the wolf.

"Very well," said the tiger, "serve me, and you shall have good food to eat."

So saying, the tiger went into his den for his nap.

When he woke up, the tiger said to the wolf, "Each day you must go to the mountain top, and see whether there are any elephants, or ponies, or buffaloes about. If you see any, come to me and say, 'Great Tiger, come forth in your might. Food is in sight'. Then I will kill and eat, and give part of the meat to you."

So day after day the wolf climbed to the mountain top, and seeing a pony, or a buffalo, or an elephant, he went back to the den, and falling at the tiger's feet he said, "Great Tiger, come forth in your might. Food is in sight."

Then the tiger would bound forth and kill whichever beast it was, sharing the meat with the wolf.

Now this wolf had never had such fine meat to eat, nor so much. So as time went on, the wolf grew bigger and bigger, and stronger and stronger, until he was really proud of his great size and strength.

"See how big and strong I am," he said to himself. "Why am I living day after day on food given to me by another? I will kill for my own eating. I will kill an elephant for myself."

So the wolf went to the tiger, and said, "I want to eat an elephant of my own killing. Will you let me lie in your corner in the den, while you climb the mountain to look out for an elephant? Then when you see one, you come to the den and say, 'Great Wolf, come forth in your might. Food is in sight'. Then I will kill the elephant."

Said the tiger, "Wolf, only tigers can kill elephants. The world has never seen a wolf that could kill an elephant. Give up this notion of yours, and eat what I kill."

But, no matter what the tiger said, the wolf would not give way. So at last the tiger said, "Well, have your

own way. Lie down in the den, and I will climb to the top of the mountain."

When he saw an elephant, the tiger went back to the mouth of the cave, and said, "Great Wolf, come forth in your might. Food is in sight."

Then from the den the wolf nimbly bounded forth, ran to where the elephant was, and, howling three times, he sprang at the elephant.

But, the wolf missed his aim, and fell down at the elephant's feet. The elephant raised his right foot and killed the wolf.

Seeing all this, the tiger said, "You will no more come forth in your might, you foolhardy wolf."

14. THE DONKEY AND THE DOG

Once upon a time, there was a man who had a dog and a donkey. One day, they were going to the market. It was a very long walk across a mountainous path. At noon, the master ate the little food he had brought along, and settled down under a tree for a nap. The donkey began to eat the grass growing there, but there was nothing for the dog to eat.

"There are some loaves among the load you are carrying," said the dog to the donkey. "Let's take one and share it between ourselves."

"O My Dear Dog! Wait till the master gets up!" said the donkey, tersely. "He'll feed you then."

Just then a ravenous wolf came into view.

"Help me, help me, dog!" pleaded the donkey, quavering in fear.

"O My Dear Donkey! I'm so hungry. I don't have the strength to do anything now," replied the dog. "Wait till the master gets up. He'll certainly help you."

15. THE TIGER AND THE DOVE

One day, while a tiger was eating his dinner, a bone stuck in his throat. It hurt so that he could not finish his dinner. He walked up and down, up and down, roaring with pain.

A dove lived on a branch of a tree nearby. Hearing the tiger, she said, "Friend, what ails you?" The tiger told the dove what the matter was, and the dove said, "I would take the bone out of your throat, friend, but I do not dare to put my head into your mouth, for fear I might never get it out again. I am afraid you might eat me."

"O Dove! Do not be afraid," the tiger said. "I will not eat you. Save my life if you can!"

"I will see what I can do for you," said the dove. "Open your mouth wide." The tiger did as he was told, but the dove said to himself. "Who knows what this tiger will do? I think I will be careful."

So the dove put a stick between the tiger's upper and lower jaws so that he could not shut his mouth.

Then the dove hopped into the tiger's mouth and hit the end of the bone with her beak. The second time she hit it, the bone fell out.

The dove hopped out of the tiger's mouth and hit the stick so that it too fell out. Then the tiger could shut his mouth.

At once the tiger felt very much better, but not one word of thanks did he say to the dove.

One day, later in the summer, the dove said to the tiger, "I want you to do something for me."

"Do something for you?" said the tiger. "You mean you want me to do something more for you. I have already done a great deal for you. You cannot expect me to do anything more for you. Do not forget that once I had you in my mouth, and I let you go. That is all that you can ever expect me to do for you."

The dove said no more, but he kept away from the tiger from that day on.

16. THE FOX AND THE OTTERS

One day, a fox said to her mate, "A longing has come upon me to eat fresh fish."

"I will go and get some for you," he said and went down to the river.

There he saw two otters standing on the bank looking for fish. Soon one of the otters saw a great fish, and entering the water, with a bound he caught hold of the tail of the fish.

But, the fish was strong and swam away, dragging the otter after him. "Come and help me," the otter called back to his friend. "This great fish will be enough for both of us!"

So the other otter went into the water. The two together were able to bring the fish to land. "Let us divide the fish into two parts."

"I want the half with the head on," said one.

"You cannot have that half. That is mine," said the other. "You take the tail."

The fox heard the otters and he went up to them.

Seeing the fox, the otters said, "O Clever One! This fish was caught by both of us together. We cannot agree about dividing it. Will you divide it for us?"

The fox cut off the tail and gave it to one, giving the head to the other. He took the large middle part for himself, saying to them, "You can eat the head and the tail without quarrelling." And away he ran with the body of the fish. The otters stood and looked at each other. They had nothing to say, but each thought to himself that the fox had run off with the best of the fish.

The fox was pleased and said to himself, as he ran towards home, "Now I have fresh fish for my mate."

His mate, seeing him coming, came to meet him, saying, "How did you get fish? You live on land, not in the water."

Then he told her of the quarrel of the otters. "I took the fish as pay for settling their quarrel," said he.

17. THE CAMEL'S CLEVERNESS

Once, there lived three animals – a goat, an ass and a camel. One day, when they were walking down a road, they found a bundle of hay that had fallen from a cart.

"This hay looks delicious," said the goat, "but it's not enough for all the three of us. Let the oldest among us have it."

"Then it is mine," said the ass. "Do you know, I was in Mysore, when Tipu was the Sultan, that makes me at least 224 years old."

"No, no, you are lying," snorted the goat. "Do you know, I was one of the animals that was driven from Delhi to Daulatabad when that madman, Sultan Muhammad bin Tughlaq shifted his capital...."

They suddenly noticed that the camel was calmly nibbling at the straw.

"What are you doing?" shouted the goat.

"Why, didn't you say the oldest should have it?" said the camel. "The two of you may be centuries old, but look at me...look at my knobby joints and wrinkled skin.....could either of you be older than me?"

And before the other two could think of a reply, the camel picked up the bundle of hay and walked away.

18. THE THREE FISHES

Once upon a time, three fishes lived in a far-away river. They were named Clever, Very-Clever, and Stupid.

One day, they left the wild country where no men lived, and came down the river to live near a town.

Very-Clever said to the other two, "There is danger all about us here. Fishermen come to the river here to catch fish with all sorts of nets and lines. Let us go back again to the wild country where we used to live."

But, the other two fishes were so lazy and so greedy that they kept putting off their going from day to day.

Then, one day Clever and Stupid went swimming on ahead of Very-Clever. They did not see the fisherman's net and rushed into it. Very-Clever saw them rush into the net.

"I must save them," said Very-Clever.

So swimming around the net, he splashed in the water in front of it, like a fish that had broken through the

net and gone up the river. Then he swam back of the net and splashed about there like a fish that had broken through and gone down the river.

The fisherman saw the splashing water and thought the fishes had broken through the net and that one had gone up the river, the other down, so he pulled in the net by one corner. That let the two fishes out of the net and away they went to find Very-Clever.

"You saved our lives, Very-Clever," they said, "and now we are willing to go back to the wild country."

So back they all went to their old home where they lived safely ever after.

19. THE KNOWLEDGEABLE FOX

Near a village, there was an enormous haystack, and several small animals had made their homes in it. Among these were a tortoise, a rabbit, a rat and a fox.

One day, as these four were enjoying a morning chat outside the haystack, the other residents came running to them in a state of panic.

"Our haystack is on fire!" they screamed.

"A fire, is it?" said the tortoise. "Please stay calm. I know a hundred thousand ways of dealing with a fire."

"And I know a thousand ways," said the rabbit, modestly.

"As for me, I know only a hundred," said the rat, "but they're all tried and trusted methods."

"And you, Sir," said the residents to the fox. "How many do you know?"

"Only one," said the fox, sniffing the smoke-laden air. "When the fire is this close there's only one thing to do: run!" And he ran away like a rocket.

"Stupid creature," sneered the tortoise. "He ran away because he has not studied fire like I or my friends here have. Listen to the first method of escaping a fire..."

But, he never got beyond that. A tongue of flame leapt out from the haystack and consumed him and his two friends. The other animals too ran for their lives like that knowledgeable fox did.

20. THE TRICKY FOX AND THE RATS

Once upon a time, a clever rat lived in the forest, and many hundreds of other rats called him their chief.

A tricky fox saw this troop of rats, and began to plan how he could catch them. He wanted to eat them, but how was he to get them? At last he thought of a plan. He went to a corner near the home of the rats and waited

until he saw one of them coming. Then he stood up on his hind legs.

The chief of the rats said to the fox, "Fox, why do you stand on your hind legs?"

"Because I am lame," said the tricky fox. "It hurts me to stand on my front legs."

"And why do you keep your mouth open?" asked the rat.

"I keep my mouth open so that I may drink in all the air I can," said the fox. "I live on air; it is my only food day after day. I cannot run or walk, so I stay here. I try not to complain."

When the rats went away, the fox lay down.

The chief of the rats was sorry for the fox, and he went each night and morning with all the other rats to talk with the fox, who seemed so poor, and who did not complain.

Each time as the rats were leaving, the fox caught and ate the last one. Then he wiped his lips, and looked as if nothing had happened.

Each night there were fewer rats at bedtime. Then they asked the chief of the rats what the trouble was. He could not be sure, but he thought the fox was to blame.

So the next day the chief said to the other rats, "You go first this time and I will go last."

They did so, and as the chief of the rats went by, the fox made a spring at him. But, the fox was not quick enough, and the chief of the rats got away.

"So this is the food you eat. Your legs are not so lame as they were. You have played your last trick, fox," said the chief of the rats, springing at the fox's throat. He bit the fox, so that he died.

And ever after the rats lived happily in peace and quiet.

21. THE TIGER AND THE FOX

Once upon a time, there was a tiger in a jungle. Once when he had gone to drink water in a stream, his feet got stuck into the wet slushy mud of the stream and he could not get out. He had to lie without food for days like that as he saw no help coming by.

One day, a kindly fox came by and dug a way out from the sand and with the extra force from the tiger helped him get out of the slush and set him free.

The tiger was grateful for this and thanked the fox for saving his life. He then offered the fox to live close to him and also promised to feed him whenever he caught food. So the fox started living with the tiger and they shared the hunt. Soon they expanded their families and had cubs and kid foxes.

After a long time, the tigress, lady of the tiger's house, grew tired of the friendship of the fox with her master. She conveyed the message to her cubs who conveyed the message to the fox kids who complained to the lady fox. The lady fox told of this to her husband. The fox went to the tiger, and told him that if he did not want the fox to stay with him, he should have told him long time back.

The tiger was surprised at this and assured the fox that no such ill-feelings existed between the tiger and the fox and assured him that he would talk to the tigress.

But, the wise fox then said, "Friend, I know you are sincere. But, our families may not exactly reciprocate the same level of friendship. So let us stay apart, and meet often as friends. But, it is better if my family stays apart from yours."

The tiger agreed to this and the two families parted as friends. The fox and the tiger were still close friends and used to go for hunting together.

22. THE FOOLISH BIRDS

Once upon a time, there was a huge tree in the forest. Many birds lived in this tree, and the wisest of them was their leader.

One day, the leader bird saw two branches rubbing against each other. Then he noticed a tiny wisp of smoke rising from the rubbing branches. He thought, "There is

no doubt a fire is starting that may burn down the whole forest."

So the wise old leader called a meeting of all the birds living in the great tree. He told them, "My dear friends, the tree we are living in, is beginning to make a fire. This fire may destroy the whole forest. Therefore, it is dangerous to stay here. Let us leave this forest at once!"

The wise birds agreed to follow his advice. So they flew away to another forest in a different land. But, the birds who were not so wise said, "That old leader panics so easily. He imagines crocodiles in a drop of water! Why should we leave our comfortable homes that have always been safe? Let the soared ones go. We will be brave and have trust in our tree!"

Lo and behold, in a little while the wise leader's warning came true. The rubbing branches made sparks that fell in the dry leaves under the tree. Those sparks became flames that grew and grew. Soon the giant tree itself caught fire. The foolish birds who still lived there were blinded and choked by the smoke. Many, who could not escape, were trapped and burned to death.

23. THE LION AND THE DEER

Once upon a time, there were two very good friends who lived together in the shade of a rock. Strange as it may seem, one was a lion and the other was a deer. They had met when they were too young to know the difference between lions and deer. So they did not think their friendship was at all unusual. Besides, it was a peaceful part of the mountains, possibly due to the influence of a gentle forest monk who lived nearby. He was a hermit, one who lives far away from other people.

For some unknown reason, one day the two friends got into a silly argument. The deer said, "Everyone knows the cold comes when the moon wanes from full to new!"

The lion said, "Where did you hear such nonsense? Everyone knows the cold comes when the moon waxes from new to full!"

The argument got stronger and stronger. Neither could convince the other. They could not reach any conclusion to resolve the growing dispute. They even started calling each other names! Fearing for their friendship, they decided to go and ask the learned forest monk, who would surely know about such thing.

Visiting the peaceful hermit, the lion and deer bowed respectfully and put their question to him. The friendly monk thought for a while and then gave his answer. "It can be cold in any phase of the moon, from new to full and back to new again. It is the wind that brings the cold, whether from west or north or east. Therefore, in a way, both of you are right! And neither of you is defeated by the other. The most important thing is to live without conflict, to remain united. Unity is best by all means."

The lion and deer thanked the wise hermit. They were happy to still be friends.

24. THE STUPID YOUNG RABBIT

O nce upon a time, there was a company of forest rabbits. In this company was a wise and respected teacher, cunning in the ways of rabbits. He taught the tricks and strategies of survival to the young rabbits.

One day, his younger sister brought her son to him, to be taught all what is important for rabbits. She said, "O brother teacher, this is my son. Please teach him the tricks and strategies of rabbits."

The teacher said to the young rabbit, "Very well, you can come at this time tomorrow for your first lesson."

At first, the young rabbit came to the lessons as he was supposed to. But, in a short time he became more interested in playing with the other young rabbits. He didn't realize how dangerous it could be for a rabbit who learned nothing but rabbit games. So he started cutting classes and enjoyed playing with the other young rabbits all the time.

Unfortunately, one day the young rabbit stepped in a snare and was trapped. Since he was missing, his mother worried. She went to her brother, the teacher, and asked him, "My dear brother, how is my son? Have you taught your nephew the tricks and strategies of rabbits?"

The teacher replied, "My dear sister, your son was disobedient and unteachable. Out of respect for you, I tried my best to teach him. But, he did not want to learn the tricks and strategies of rabbits. He played with the other young rabbits all the time! How could I possibly teach him? You are obedient and faithful, but he is not. It is useless to try to teach him."

Later they heard the sad news; the stubborn young rabbit had been trapped and killed by a hunter.

❀ ❀ ❀

25. THE HUMBLE SWAN AND THE BOASTFUL CROW

Once upon a time, there lived many swans near a beach. One day, when they were flying down, a crow watched them with disdain.

"How gracelessly you fly!" he said to the swans. "All you know is how to flap your wings. Can you glide? Can you somersault in the air? No, that's beyond you. Let's have a flying contest. I'll show you what flying really is!"

One of the swans, a young, sturdy male, took up the challenge, whereupon the crow flew up and began to display his flying prowess. He flew in circles, swooped down like an arrow, and performed a variety of acrobatics in the air. Then he flew down, cawing triumphantly.

Now it was the swan's turn. He launched himself into the air and began flying over the sea. The crow flew after

him, making all sorts of derisive comments about his manner of flying. On and on they flew till finally the land was lost to sight. Water stretched endlessly on all sides. The crow's comments became less and less frequent and finally, stopped altogether. He had begun to tire. Eventually he became so tired that he found it hard to stay in the air. He had to struggle to keep from falling into the water.

The swan, pretending to be unaware of his plight, said, "Why do you keep touching the water, brother? Is that another flying manoeuvre?"

"No," squawked the crow, the fight completely gone out of him. "I'm in trouble... a curse on my boasting! If you do not come to my aid, I'll drown!"

The swan had pity on him and taking him on his back flew back to the shore.

26. CHARLIE FOX AND THE ROOSTER

"Hey Rooster," yelped the fox, "Fly out of that chicken yard and play with me."

"Are you crazy, fox? I know what you want," crowed rooster.

"The farmer said if I behave and don't hurt any of you, we can be friends," smiled the fox.

"You are not telling the truth, so just go back home and find some other friends," the rooster said as he walked back to the hens.

"What did Charlie the fox want?" clucked all of the hens, together.

After the rooster told them the latest story Charlie the fox told, all of the hens fluttered in fright.

"Do you think the humans told the fox we could play with Charlie?" a little baby chick said.

"Maybe the fox has changed," crowed a young rooster, "I sure would like to see some new places."

"Sure!" crowed the rooster, fluffing his feathers, "Have you ever wondered whatever happened to others, like you, when they fell for Charlie the fox's lies?"

"Now listen to me, you dumb chickens, Charlie the fox is just telling you all lies, the farmer would never let anything happen to us, remember you hens feed him eggs every morning," lectured the rooster.

The next day Charlie the fox and a couple of his friends came back again.

"Hey Rooster! Look, whom I have brought. We want to be friends, come out and play," shouted Charlie.

The rooster strolled over to the fence and whispered, "Next time you come here and don't tell the truth, the farmer will come and send all of you to another country." The rooster walked back to the rest of the flock.

Charlie and his friends ran away laughing, "Boy, those chickens are dumb, how will the farmer find out about us, Hahaha."

After the chickens were fed that night, the rooster and hens worked out a plan to get all of the foxes in trouble with their friend, the farmer.

The next day, again, Charlie the fox and his friends came back, surrounding the chicken yard, trying to scare the chickens, hoping one of them would fly out of the yard.

The rooster crowed, loudly, "Now, everyone!"

All of the chickens flopped around, crashing into fences, clucking as loud as they could at the top of their beaks. The fox couldn't figure out what was going on.

Just then the screen door, on the house, swing open. The farmer, with his shotgun in his hands, ran out, shouting at the top of his voice, "What is going on out there?"

The farmer saw Charlie the fox and his friends and shot his gun over their heads. "Get out of here or you guys will be eating lead for supper."

As Charlie ran away with his friends following behind, the rooster crowed as loud as he could, "Hey Charlie, if you don't tell the truth, you pay the consequences." All of the chickens cheeped with happiness.

27. THE HALF-EDUCATED JACKAL

One day, a wolf met a jackal and asked him, "How far have you studied?"

"I'm only half-educated," said the jackal.

"Then I'm twice as educated as you," said the wolf. "From now on you should address me as 'Sir'."

Just then a ferocious tiger stepped out from behind a bush.

"What shall we do, Sir?" asked the jackal.

But, the wolf was so frightened that he couldn't talk.

"Going somewhere?" growled the tiger, positioning himself to leap.

"We were in fact coming to consult you, Sir," said the jackal, thinking quickly. "A dispute has arisen between us and only you with your superior intelligence could settle it for us."

The tiger was pleased.

"What's this dispute about?" he asked, relaxing.

"I have caught two plump chickens," said the jackal. "My friend says that as he is more educated than me he should get one!"

"How far have you studied?" asked the tiger, looking the wolf up and down.

The wolf's teeth chattered in fright.

"He says he has as many qualifications as there are teeth in his mouth," interpreted the jackal.

"Is that so?" asked the tiger. "Then I'm far better educated... see!" And he opened his mouth to show his fearsome teeth.

The sight so unnerved the wolf that his legs gave way and he fell flat on his face.

"He admits you're more educated and is prostrating at your teeth," explained the jackal. "I should prostrate too for the wisdom you've shown in settling our dispute."

"I have?" said the tiger, perplexed.

"Now that you've claimed the chickens for yourself, my friend and I no longer have a dispute," said the jackal. "Please follow me to my house and I'll give you the chickens."

The tiger was delighted. He rarely got to eat chicken. Also, his superior intelligence told him that once he had eaten the chickens there was nothing to prevent him from eating the jackal and the wolf too.

"Lead the way," he said.

The jackal led him to the mouth of a tunnel in the side of a hill.

"Here we are," he said. "My friend will go in and bring the chickens."

The opening was much too small for the wolf, but he was so eager to gain the safety of the tunnel that he somehow squeezed himself through it.

When he did not come out for some time, the jackal said he would see what was keeping him and deftly slipped into the tunnel too.

It took some time for the tiger to realise that he had been tricked. Then he was so furious that he forgot he was educated and putting his face close to the opening roundly cursed the jackal and flung the choicest abuses at him.

After he had gone, the wolf, helped by the jackal, squeezed out of the tunnel.

He had got his voice back.

"You may be half-educated," he said admiringly, "but you've certainly got brains."

"Thank you," said the jackal, "Sir!"

28. THE CROOKED TOWN MOUSE

One day, a mouse living in the town met a mouse which lived in the field. "Where do you come from?" asked the latter when she saw the town mouse.

"I come from yonder town," replied the town mouse.

"How is life going there with you?"

"Very well, indeed. I am living in the lap of luxury. Whatever I want of sweets or any other good things is found in abundance in my master's house. But, how are you living?"

"I have nothing to complain of. You just come and see my stores. I have grain and nuts, and all the fruits of the tree and field in my storehouse."

The town mouse did not quite believe the story of his new friend, and, driven by curiosity, went with him to the latter's house. How great was his surprise when he found that the field mouse had spoken the truth; his garner was full of nuts and grain and other stores, and his mouth watered when he saw all the riches which were stored up there.

Then he turned to the field mouse and said, "Oh, yes, you have here a nice snug place and something to live upon, but you should come to my house and see what I have there. Your stock is nothing compared with the riches which are mine."

The field mouse, who was rather simple by nature and trusted his new friend, went with him into the town to see what better things the other could have. He had never been into the town and did not know what his friend could mean when he boasted of his greater riches. So they went together, and the town mouse took his friend to his master's house. He was a grocer, and there were boxes and sacks full of every good thing the heart of a mouse could desire. When he saw all these riches, the field mouse said he could never have believed it, had he not seen it with his own eyes.

While they were talking together, a cat came in. As soon as the town mouse saw the cat, he slipped quietly behind a box and hid himself. His friend, who had never yet seen a cat, turned to him and asked who that gentleman was who had come in so quietly.

"Don't you know who he is? He is our priest, and he has come to see us. You must go and pay your respects to him and kiss his hand. See what a beautiful glossy coat he has on, and how his eyes sparkle, and how demurely he keeps his hands in the sleeves of his coat."

Not suspecting anything, the field mouse did as he was told and went up to the cat. The cat gave him at once her blessing, and the mouse had no need of another after that. The cat gave him extreme unction there and then. That was just what the town mouse had intended. When he saw how well stored the home of the field mouse was, he had made up his mind to trap him and to kill him, so that he might take possession of all that the field mouse had gathered up. He had learned the ways of the townspeople and had acted accordingly.

29. THE DOG AND THE DOLPHIN

Once upon a time, some sailors set out to sea in their sailing ship. One of them brought his pet dog along for the long journey.

When they were far out at sea, a terrible storm overturned their ship. Everyone in the ship drowned, and the dog was sure that he would drown. Suddenly a kind dolphin appeared and picked him up.

They soon reached an island and the dog came down from the dolphin's back. The dolphin asked the dog, "Do you know this place?"

The dog replied, "Yes, I do. In fact, the King of this island is my best friend. Do you know that I am actually a prince?"

Knowing that no one lived on that island, the dolphin said, "Well, well, so you are a prince! Now you can be a King!"

The dog asked, "How can I be a King?"

As the dolphin started swimming away, he answered, "That is easy. As you are the only creature on this island, you will naturally be the King!"

✹ ✹ ✹

30. THE TORTOISE AND THE BIRDS

There was a famine one time that went on for months. Even tortoise, who was slow but cunning and full of tricks, had not had a good meal for two months. He could walk a little faster because his body had shrunken so, but that was of no use if he was weak from hunger and there was little food to be found. As tortoise crept about, he listened carefully for news of food. He only heard of a feast that the sky-gods were preparing for their friends, the birds. The feast was to be in the sky itself, where only the birds and the sky-gods could go.

The tortoise thought for a long time about how to get some of the feast. He then went to some birds and said, "I wish that I could see this wonderful place where you are going."

"Ah, tortoise," laughed the birds. "We would gladly help you, but we know that you are full of tricks and that we shall be sorry if we do."

The tortoise replied, "What use is trickery if one is starving and there is no food? I have learned my lesson – tricks go back on the trickster. I am a changed tortoise." He kept talking to the birds, who were of good heart and wanted to believe him, till at last they agreed to help.

Each bird gave a few feathers and they stuck them onto the tortoise till he was covered with feathers of many colours. He found that he could flap his arms like wings and that he could fly. The birds went with him into the air and showed him the way to the place of the sky-gods' feast. As they went, the tortoise said, "I have heard that the sky-gods have a custom now. When they have a feast, everyone who is invited must have a new name. My name shall be 'All of You.'"

The birds were confused, but they knew that the tortoise was wise and heard many new things as he crept all over the land. They decided to believe him.

When they arrived at the place of the feast, the sky-gods set out much to eat and drink. The sky-gods needed to leave before the feasting started, but before they left, the tortoise asked them, "Who is all this for?"

"This is for all of you," answered the sky-gods.

The tortoise turned and said to the birds, "You have heard them. My new name is 'All of You'. This is all for me. If there is any left after I am done, you may have it."

The angry birds watched as the tortoise devoured everything. Not a scrap or drop was left. Soon they all flew down to the Earth. The birds wanted to punish the crooked tortoise, but they decided to wait a while first.

Much later, nothing had been said about the tortoise's trick. The tortoise thought that the birds had accepted that he was cleverer than they, and had chosen to do nothing. Later still, he heard of another feast for the birds. "Is this another feast of the sky-gods?" he inquired of some birds.

"No," they replied. "This one is on the ground, not far from here. You may come, if you promise no more trickery." Of course the tortoise agreed. The birds told him how to get to the place of feasting.

They all gathered before the food and drink. A bird announced that no one could eat until his or her claws were clean. Everyone rushed to a nearby stream to wash. The birds flew back to the feast, but the tortoise had to crawl along the ground. When he got back to the food, his claws were dirty again. He kept going back to the stream, but he could not keep his claws from getting dirty. The tortoise realized he had been tricked by the birds. He had to watch and listen while the birds feasted. When they were done, they had not left a scrap or drop for the tortoise.

The birds flew away, making fun of the tortoise as they left with full stomachs.

31. THE RABBIT'S MOTHER

Once there was a place far away, where there were only animals and plants. There was enough food for everyone, but the animals had grown selfish and greedy. They held a meeting to talk about what might happen if there was not enough food for everyone. No one could think of what to do. Finally one animal suggested that they should keep other animals away and keep all the food for themselves. For a long time, any animal that wandered into this land was chased away.

The animals might have been satisfied with this, but they noticed that there were more animals than ever. This was because the mothers among them were still having babies. Another meeting was held to worry about the food supply. Some crafty and cruel animals said that the mothers should stop having babies. Another proposed that all the mothers be killed so that there would be no babies. That night, all the selfish animals killed their own mothers, except for the rabbit.

Some of the animals had thought that the plan to kill their mothers was wrong, but the largest and fiercest animals had threatened to punish anyone who did not go along with the others. The rabbit saw that there was no way to stop the others, and quietly carried out his plan to save his mother. He cut a thick leaf into the shape of his mother and covered it with a skin. The next morning he dragged the leaf to the meeting place with the other animals. Staying in the shadows of the largest animals, he tossed the leaf into the burial pit just underneath the falling body of the lion's mother. No one noticed the trick.

The rabbit had hidden his mother in a small cave. She had made a door with a catch on it that only she knew to undo. Everyday the rabbit would go to the cave and make a certain sound. His mother knew the sound and her son's voice. She would undo the catch, open the door, and the two would share a fine meal.

As the months went by, the other animals grew hungrier. They had no mothers to make meals for them or to show them how to cook for themselves. With no mothers to plant and tend gardens, they had to live on whatever nuts and berries they could find. Only the rabbit remained fat and sleek while the others grew thinner and sadder.

One day, the animals had another meeting while the rabbit was away. They decided to find out his secret. The fly was sent to follow him. The next day the fly never let the rabbit out of its sight. Hiding under a leaf, the fly saw the rabbit come to the cave and make the sound his mother knew. As the fly flew through the open door after the rabbit, the rabbit's mother saw it. The fly promised to keep the secret if the rabbits would share their food with it. The fly was given a generous portion, but as soon as it was done it flew straight back to the other animals and told them everything.

Instead of learning from the rabbit's wisdom and their own terrible deed, the animals became angry and decided to punish the rabbit by killing its mother. The fly led them to the cave. The door was too small for the larger animals to tear down, and too well made for the smaller animals to open. The animals tried to make the sound that the mother knew, but she recognized their voices. Finally the animals hid themselves and made Robin try. Robin was the rabbit's cousin and their voices were the same. The mother opened the door and was killed.

The rabbit came back from searching for another hiding place. He cried for a long time when he saw his mother's torn and crushed body. Then he buried it near the cave.

Not wanting to ever see the other animals again, the rabbit lived in the cave. As the months went by, a tree grew from the grave. He liked to sit underneath it and pretend that the tree had his mother's spirit. He would talk to it as if his mother could hear what he was saying.

On one hot and sunny day, he playfully said, "It is so hot that I wish you were bigger, so you could give more shade."

To his astonishment, in a few minutes the tree had grown another foot. Soon he discovered that the tree would give him any kind of fruit he asked for.

It was not long before the other animals found out that the rabbit had grown fat again. Throughout the whole countryside, the food supply was nearly gone. The animals were too hungry to think of being cruel to the rabbit. The fly was sent again to find out the secret.

Soon the fly returned with its discovery. "The rabbit has an enchanted tree. It gives him shade and whatever food he wants." The animals did not want to risk losing such a supply of food. Knowing that the tree might obey only the rabbit, they came to the rabbit and pretended to be ashamed of all they had done. They begged his forgiveness and asked for his friendship.

The rabbit was kind, but did not trust the others. He gave them all food from the tree each day. He asked the tree to stay short but to grow wide, so that the animals could all climb into its branches to eat. One day, he saw that all the animals were in the tree and on its branches; even the mighty elephant was on the thickest branch.

The rabbit whispered to the tree. Suddenly the trunk grew taller so quickly that before the animals could jump away, they found themselves above the clouds. Then the tree shook itself so violently that all the animals were thrown to their deaths. Even the fly was killed as a rat held onto it, trying desperately to keep from falling.

Now the rabbit was alone with the spirit of his mother. It was not long before he told the story to the animals in the surrounding lands, and they came to live in peace with each other in the place the selfish animals had tried to keep for themselves.

32. THE CLEVER LAMB

A lamb was grazing with a flock of sheep one day. She soon found some sweet grass at the edge of the field. Farther and farther she went, away from the others.

She was enjoying herself so much that she did not notice a wolf coming nearer to her. However, when it pounced on her, she thought fast and pleaded, "Please, please don't eat me yet. My stomach is full of grass. If you wait a while, I will taste much better."

The wolf thought that was a good idea, so he sat down and waited. After a while, the lamb said, "If you allow me to dance, the grass in my stomach will be digested faster."

Again the wolf agreed.

While the lamb was dancing, she had a new idea. She said, "Please take the bell from around my neck. If you ring it as hard as you can, I will be able to dance even faster."

The wolf took the bell and rang it as hard as he could. The shepherd heard the bell ringing and quickly sent his dogs to find the missing lamb. The barking dogs frightened the wolf away and saved the lamb's life.

33. THE DEER AND THE FARMER

Once there was a deer who loved to eat the fruits and roots and shoots of the forest. But, he loved something else even more.

He loved the vegetables in the farmer's garden.

One day, the deer went to the edge of the forest. He looked out at row after row of vegetables.

"Juicy cucumbers!" said the deer and he got into the garden.

"Oh!"

His leg was caught in a snare! Deer pulled and pulled. But, he could not get away.

"Oh, no!" he said. "The farmer will have me for dinner!"

Then he saw the farmer coming. The deer thought fast. He lay on the ground and made his body stiff.

"Well, well," said the farmer. "Look what I caught. A deer! But, he looks dead."

The farmer pushed him with his foot. The deer didn't move.

"Maybe he's been dead a long time," said the farmer. "Too bad! I guess we can't eat him."

He pulled the deer's leg out of the snare. Then he tossed the deer back into the forest.

The deer landed with a soft plop. Then he jumped up and ran. Behind him, he heard the farmer yell.

"Hey! You tricked me!"

The deer laughed. "The farmer is smart. But, the deer is smarter!"

A few days passed. The deer kept thinking about all those vegetables. One day, he went back to the edge of the forest.

"Tasty gourds! Scrumptious sweet potatoes!" said the deer.

Then he saw something new. It looked like a man. But, its head was a coconut, and its body was rubber.

"A scarecrow!" said the deer. "That silly farmer. Does he think he can scare me with that? I'll show him how scared I am!"

The deer marched up to the scarecrow. "Take this!" He gave it a big kick.

But, his leg stuck to the scarecrow. The scarecrow

was covered with sticky sap from a rubber tree!

"Let me go!" said the deer. He pulled and he pulled. Then he pushed with his other front leg.

That leg stuck too.

"Turn me loose!" He pulled and he pulled. Then he pushed with his two back legs.

They stuck too.

"Put me down!" He pulled and he pushed and he pulled and he pushed. But, the deer was trapped.

Then he saw the farmer. Deer thought fast. But, he didn't have any ideas!

"Well, well," said the farmer. "How nice of you to come back."

He pulled the deer off the scarecrow and carried him to the house. He put him outside in an empty chicken coop.

"I'll keep you here tonight," said the farmer. "And tomorrow you'll be our dinner."

All that night, the deer couldn't sleep. He didn't want to be dinner! When the sun rose, the deer just lay there sadly.

Then he heard something. "Why, it's the deer! So the farmer caught you at last. It serves you right!"

It was the farmer's dog. The deer thought fast.

"What do you mean, dog? The farmer didn't catch me."

"Then why are you in the coop?" said the dog.

"Because there aren't enough beds in the house. You see, the farmer is holding a feast tomorrow. And I'm the Guest of Honour."

"Guest of Honour?" said the dog. "That's not fair! I've been his loyal friend for years, and you're just a thief. I should be the Guest of Honour!"

"You know, dog, you're right. Why don't you take my place? When the farmer sees you in this coop, he'll make you the Guest of Honour instead."

"Really?" said the dog. "You don't mind?"

"Not at all," said the deer. "You deserve it."

"Deer, you're not so bad after all. Thank you!" The dog lifted the latch and opened the door.

"You're welcome, dog. Enjoy the feast."

The deer ran towards the forest. Then he watched from the forest edge. He saw the farmer come out and stare at the dog. Then he heard the farmer yell.

"You stupid dog! You let the deer get away!"

The deer laughed. "Farmer will have to find a different dinner now!" Then he went off singing his song.

"I'm quick and smart as I can be. Try and try, but you can't catch me!"

34. THE CUNNING ROOSTERS

Once upon a time, roosters ruled cats. The cats worked hard all day and at night they had to bring all they had gathered for the roosters. The King of the roosters would take all the food for himself and for the other roosters.

The roosters loved to eat ants. Thus, every cat had a purse hung round its neck, which it filled with ants for the King of the roosters.

The cats did not like the situation. They wanted to rid themselves of the King so that the food they gathered through hard work and great difficulty would be their own. But, they were afraid of the roosters.

The roosters had told the cats that roosters' combs were made out of fire and that the fire of their combs would burn anyone who disobeyed them! The cats believed them and therefore worked from early morning until late night for the roosters.

One night, the fire on the house of Mrs. Cat went out. She told her kitten, Softy, to bring some fire from Mr. Rooster's house.

When Softy went into the house of the rooster, she saw that Mr. Rooster was fast asleep, his stomach swollen with the ants he had eaten. The kitten was afraid to wake the rooster, so she returned home empty handed and told her mother what had happened.

Mrs. Cat said, "Now that the rooster is asleep, gather some dry twigs and place them near his comb. As soon as the twigs catch fire, bring them home."

Softy gathered some dry twigs and took them to the rooster's house. He was still asleep. Softy fearfully put the dry twigs near the rooster's comb, but it was no use, the twigs did not catch fire. Softy rubbed the twigs against the rooster's comb again, but it was no use, they would not catch fire.

Softy returned home without any fire and told her mother, "The rooster's comb does not set twigs on fire."

Mrs. Cat answered, "Why can't you do anything right! Come with me. I'll show you how to make fire with the rooster's comb."

So, together they went to the house of Mr. Rooster.

He was still asleep. Mrs. Cat put the twigs as near to the rooster's comb as she could. But, the twigs did not

catch fire. Then, shaking with fear, she put her paw near the rooster's comb and gently touched it. To her surprise, the comb was not hot, it was very cold. It was just red coloured!

As soon as Mrs. Cat realized that the roosters had lied to the cats about their combs, she joyfully went out and told the other cats about the rooster's tricks. From that day on, the cats no longer worked for the roosters.

At first, the King of the roosters became very angry and said to the cats, "I will burn all of your houses, if you do not work for me!"

But, the cats said, "Your comb is not made of fire. It is just the colour of fire. We touched it, when you were fast asleep. You lied to us."

When the King of the roosters found out that the cats knew he had lied to them, he ran away. Now, whenever roosters see a cat, they scurry away, because to this very day they are afraid of cats.

35. THE FOOLISH LION

A deer was grazing on a grassy plain. As she slowly walked about, she saw a lion in a cage nearby. She started to run away, but the lion motioned for her to come nearer. She saw that the lion was starving and exhausted. The cage was locked.

"Please help me and unlock this cage," begged the lion. "I have been left here and do not know if anyone will return. I have no food or water."

The trembling deer answered, "I am afraid that I shall be your first meal." But, the lion kept pleading and promised to leave the deer alone. The deer was kind of heart, and could not bear to leave the lion to die a slow and terrible death. She unlocked the cage and opened the door.

The lion stepped out and thanked the deer. As the deer turned and left, the lion took a few steps and realized that he was weaker than he had thought. Thinking that he might not be able to catch anything else, he ignored his promise and pounced upon the deer.

"Is this my reward for my kindness to you? Was I wrong to help you?" asked the deer. Just then a clever man came walking by and asked what the deer had meant. The lion stepped away from the deer and the deer explained her version of what had happened. The lion then said that he was only doing what he could to stay alive, since he was not sure he would have been able to find any other food.

"I do not understand all of this," said the man. "Is this the cage?" The animals said that it was so. "How were you sitting in this cage?" he asked the lion.

"Like this," the lion lay down and showed him. The man got into the cage and crouched within it.

"This is the way you were lying in the cage?" he asked.

"No," replied the lion. The man got out and the lion got in, again showing how he had been sitting. The man quickly locked the cage.

"This is the reward for the ungrateful," called out the man as he and the deer left, leaving the lion wondering if anyone else would ever come along to help him.

36. THE STUPID DOG

Once upon a time, there was a dog that was looking for something to eat. He was very, very hungry. No matter how hard the dog tried, he could not find food. Finally, he went to the edge of the forest and searched there for food. Suddenly, he caught sight of a big tree with a hole in it.

Inside the hole was a package. The hungry dog immediately thought that there might be food in it, and he became very happy. He jumped into the hole and when he opened the package, he saw there were a lot of food, bread, meat and fruit in it!

An old woodcutter had placed the food in the tree trunk while he was cutting down trees in the forest. He was going to eat it for his lunch.

The dog happily began to eat. After the dog had finished eating, he felt thirsty and decided to leave the trunk and drink some water from a nearby spring. However, no matter how hard he tried, he could not get out of the hole. Do you know why? Yes, the dog had eaten so much food that he became too big to come out through the hole.

The dog was very sad and upset. He told himself, "I wish that I had thought a little before jumping into the hole."

37. THE PEACEMAKERS

The leaders of the tigers, the wolves and the deer met to find a way to ensure that their three groups always lived together in peace. They began the meeting by agreeing that the leaders themselves should set the example of friendship with each other.

"To make sure that we do not offend one another," said the tiger, "let us tell each other what we dislike, so that we may not hurt each other accidentally." The others agreed that this was a good idea.

"Only one thing bothers me, but I hate it," said the deer. "I do not want to be talked about when I am away."

The wolf said, "Being talked about does not bother me, but I do not like it when anyone steps on my tail."

"None of those things affect me," said the tiger, "but I hate it when anyone looks at me without respect."

As peacemakers, they agreed to remember what had been said and not to offend each other, as well as teach what they had learned to the animals they represented. The deer excused himself to run an errand.

When the deer had left, the tiger asked the wolf, "I wonder what the deer thinks we say about him when he is not with us?"

"Probably how clumsy he looks because of his short tail and stick-like legs," laughed the wolf.

The deer had never left, but had hidden behind the bush to listen to the others. Pretending to come back from his errand, he gave the tiger a dirty look. The tiger, angered at the way the deer had scowled at him, began to fight with the deer. As they fought, the tiger stepped on the wolf's tail and then the three of them started fighting.

By this time, the rest of the wolves, tigers and deer had come to see how their leaders were doing and all three groups joined in the fray.

38. THE LION AND THE CRANE

A great and fearsome lion went out for hunting. It was not long before he caught and killed a zebra that was big enough for his lioness and cubs to eat their fill, with plenty left over for himself. When he and his family were eating, a small bone got caught in the great lion's throat. He could barely squeak to his lioness that a bone was caught in his throat.

The lioness tried to get the bone out with her paw, but she could not get her great paw far enough into the lion's mouth. The cubs could get to his throat with their little paws, but they were too clumsy to get the bone out.

Soon the lion saw a crane sitting on a high branch watching him. "Crane," squeaked the lion. "Help your King. Your neck is long and thin and so is your beak. You can take out this bone from my throat."

The crane was in no hurry. "Why would I do that? One bite and both the bone and I will be in your stomach."

"I shall reward you," said the lion. "I do not want you both stuck in my throat. Then who would help me?"

The greedy crane could not resist the promise of a reward. He flew down to the lion and ordered, "Open your mouth as wide as you can." With the lioness and cubs watching, the lion opened his mouth wide. The crane stuck its bill down the lion's throat until its whole head and part

of its neck were in the lion's mouth. The bone was easily plucked out and dropped at the lion's feet.

"I'll have that reward now," said the crane.

"You already have it," said the lion. "Now you can tell the other animals that you gave an order to your King and he obeyed. You can boast that you put your head into a lion's mouth and lived to tell of it."

The crane started to argue, but even the mighty elephant knows better than to argue with a group of lions. Amid the roars all around him, he stretched his wings and flew away to tell his story, as far from any lions as possible.

39. WHY THE BEAR HAS A SHORT TAIL?

Once upon a time, the bear had a long bushy tail. And every time he would see the fox, he would shake and wave his tail in the fox's face. The fox studied and studied how to get even with the bear. One day, he went to fishing and he had good luck. As he was coming home from fishing, the bear came and said, "Brother fox, how did you catch all these fish?"

The fox said to himself, "Now's my time to get even with the bear." Then he said, "Any cold night, all you got to do is to go down to the creek and hang your tail in the

water, and let it hang there from sundown to sunup the next morning, and you'll have more fish than you can pull out."

He meant that the bear's tail would freeze in the ice. "All right," said the bear, "I believe that I'll go fishing tonight." So he went at night, and sat on a log with his tail in the water in the middle of the creek. It grew so cold that he began to shiver. All night he sat there and thought about the fish he would have in the morning.

Next morning the sun began to rise, so the bear tried to pull his fish. But, his tail was frozen too tight in the ice. He pulled and he pulled, but his tail was stuck fast. The bear began to be afraid that men would come along and see him. So he pulled his tail with all his might, and off came the bear's tail, but it was cut and too short. So, the bear has been having a short tail ever since from that day to this.

40. THE COUNTRY MOUSE AND THE TOWN MOUSE

One day, a town mouse went to pay a visit to his cousin in the country. The country mouse was rough, but he loved his town friend and made him heartily welcome. Beans and bacon, cheese and bread, were all he had to offer, but he offered them freely.

The town mouse rather turned up his long nose at this country fare, and said, "I cannot understand, cousin, how you can put up with such poor food as this, but of course you cannot expect anything better in the country. You come with me and I will show you how to live. When you have been in town a week, you will wonder how you could ever have stood a country life."

When the country mouse heard this from the town mouse, he agreed to come to the town with him. Immediately, the two mice set off for the town and arrived at the town mouse's residence late at night.

"You may want some refreshment after our long journey," said the polite town mouse, and took his friend into the grand dining room.

There they found the remains of a fine feast, and soon the two mice were eating up jellies and cakes and all that was nice. Suddenly they heard growling and barking.

"What is that?" said the country mouse.

"It is only the dogs of the house," answered the other.

"Only!" said the country mouse. "I do not like that music at my dinner." Just at that moment the door flew open, in came two huge mastiffs, and the two mice had to scamper down and run off. "Good-bye, cousin," said the country mouse.

"What! Going so soon?" asked the town mouse.

"Yes," he replied. "Better beans and bacon in peace than cakes and all in fear."

41. THE DIRTY DEER

The lion had had a good day at hunting and had eaten to his heart's content. Now he wanted a drink of water and so made his way to a pool.

A young deer was drinking at the pool and when he saw the lion approaching, froze in terror. But, the lion ignored him and bent to drink, only to recoil in disgust - the water smelt foul.

He decided to go to another pool. The deer, puzzled by his behaviour, jumped to the conclusion that the lion was going away without drinking, out of fear of him.

Suddenly feeling as strong as an elephant, he ran after the lion and challenged him to a fight.

"Not today," said the lion, looking over his shoulder. "Meet me here tomorrow and we'll fight."

The deer took his reluctance to fight as further evidence of his fear of him and his spirits soared.

He rushed home and began to boast that soon he would be King of the jungle instead of the lion.

When his family and friends heard he had challenged the lion, they were appalled. They guessed why the lion had turned away from the pool, and took the deer to task for his foolish action.

The deer soon realised that he had made a terrible mistake and was seized by a cold panic. Seeing his distress, his aged grandfather hastily worked out a plan to save him.

"Keep your appointment with the lion," he advised his grandson, "otherwise he will come here looking for you and slaughter us all. But, before going to meet him, roll in the dirt and mud so that you stink to high heaven."

Came the day of the big fight. The deer rolled in the mud and in elephant's dung and in all the other rubbish he could find and then went to meet the lion.

The lion was waiting impatiently for him, but when the deer drew near, stepped back in disgust.

"What have you done to yourself?" he snarled. "You...you stink! Yeecch!"

He had come with the thought of feasting on delicious deer meat, but now he felt nauseated and his appetite vanished.

"I've come to fight," squeaked the deer, stepping forward.

"Get away from me!" growled the lion. "Go!"

The deer turned and ran to safety.

42. TIGER GOES ABROAD

Once in a village, there lived a beautiful dog which had black spots on its body. Its name was 'Tiger'.

When a lengthy famine set in, the dogs and other animals began to leave their families. Tiger, whose throat was emaciated with hunger, was driven to another country.

There, in a certain city, he went to a certain house day after day where, due to the carelessness of the housekeeper, many good things to eat were left lying about, and he ate his fill.

However, upon leaving the house, other vicious dogs chased and surrounded him on all sides and tore into him on all parts of his body with their teeth.

Then he reconsidered his situation, and thought, "It is better at home. Even during a famine I can live there in peace, and no one will bite me to pieces. I will return to my own village."

Having thought thus, it set forth to his own village. When he arrived there, all of his relatives asked him, "Tiger, tell us about where you have been. What is the

country like? How do the people behave? What do they eat? What do they do?"

Tiger answered, "How can I explain to you the essence of a foreign place? There are good things to eat in great variety, and kind-hearted housekeepers who do not keep watch! But, the only one evil in a foreign country is dogs."

43. THE FOOLISH LEOPARD

Once there was a deer in a forest. He was looking for tasty fruits and roots and shoots.

Though he was small, he was not afraid. He knew that many big animals wanted to eat him. But, first they had to catch him!

Then he heard something. Rowr!

There was a leopard!

"Hello, deer. I was just getting hungry. Now you can be my lunch."

The deer didn't want to be lunch. He looked around and thought fast. He saw a mud puddle.

"I'm sorry, leopard. I can't be your lunch. The King has ordered me to guard his pudding."

"His pudding?" said the leopard.

"Yes. There it is." The deer pointed to the mud puddle. "It has the best taste in the world. The King doesn't want anyone else to eat it."

The leopard looked longingly at the puddle. "I would like to taste the King's pudding."

"Oh, no, leopard! The King would be very angry."

"Just one little taste, deer! The King will never know."

"Well, all right, leopard. But, first let me run far away, so no one will blame me."

"All right, deer, you can go now."

The deer ran quickly out of sight.

"Imagine!" said the leopard. "The King's pudding!" He took a big mouthful.

Then he spit it out.

"Oh! That's no pudding. That's mud!"

The leopard ran through the forest. He caught up with the deer.

"Deer, you tricked me once. But, now you will be my lunch!"

The deer looked around and thought fast. He saw a wasp nest in a tree.

"I'm sorry, leopard. I can't be your lunch. The King has ordered me to guard his drum."

"His drum?" said the leopard.

"Yes. There it is." The deer pointed to the wasp nest. "It has the best sound in the world. The King doesn't want anyone else to hit it."

The leopard said, "I would like to hit the King's drum."

"Oh, no, leopard! The King would be very angry."

"Just one little hit, deer! The King will never know."

"Well, all right, leopard. But, first let me run far away, so no one will blame me."

"All right, deer, you can go now."

The deer ran quickly out of sight.

"Imagine!" said the leopard. "The King's drum!" He reached up and hit it.

The wasps all flew out. They started to sting the leopard.

"Oh! That's no drum. That's a wasp nest!"

The leopard ran away. But, the wasps only followed him!

The leopard came to a stream. He jumped in and stayed underwater as long as he could. At last the wasps went away.

Then the leopard jumped out. He ran through the forest till he found the deer.

"Deer, you tricked me once. You tricked me twice. But, now you will be my lunch!"

The deer looked around and thought fast. He saw a cobra! The giant snake was coiled asleep on the ground.

"I'm sorry, leopard. I can't be your lunch. The King has ordered me to guard his belt."

"His belt?" said the leopard.

"Yes. There it is." The deer pointed to the cobra. "It's the best belt in the world. The King doesn't want anyone else to wear it."

The leopard said, "I would like to wear the King's belt."

"Oh, no leopard! The King would be very angry."

"Just for one moment, deer! The King will never know."

"Well, all right, leopard. But, first let me run far away, so no one will blame me."

"All right, deer, you can go now."

The deer ran quickly out of sight.

"Imagine!" said the leopard. "The King's belt!" He started to wrap it around himself.

The cobra woke up. It didn't wait for the leopard to finish wrapping. It wrapped itself around the leopard. Then it squeezed him and bit him.

"Oh! That's no belt. That's a cobra! Help deer! Help!"

But, the deer was far away.

44. THE CLEVER SPARROW

Once upon a time, an argument arose among the birds as to who could fly the highest. The smaller birds became quiet, for no one else listened to them anyway. It was the larger birds who boasted and argued. It was decided to hold a flying contest, after a few weeks of training for all the birds who wished to participate.

The smaller birds did not think they had a chance, and did not bother to strengthen their wings. This was except for the sparrow, who was aware of how small and weak she was. She tried to think of how she could win through trickery, and finally hatched a plan.

On the day of the contest, almost all the birds were saying that the eagle would win. The eagle was a swift, strong bird who spent each day flying higher than most birds did. The sparrow heard what the others were saying, and decided to stay as close to the eagle as she could. The

birds swooped into the air and towards the clouds. It was not long before some of them began to fall behind. The sparrow managed to keep near the eagle.

Soon the birds soared into a cloud. The sparrow was so small and light that the eagle never noticed when she softly landed on the eagle's back.

As the two passed upwards through the cloud, the other birds saw what had happened and cheered for the sparrow.

The eagle thought that they were cheering for him, and beat his wings more strongly to show off. As he rose higher and higher, he called to the others he was leaving behind, "Who is flying the highest?"

"I am," said a tiny voice from above him.

The eagle was astonished. He flew higher and asked again, "Who is flying the highest?"

"I am," the sparrow answered again.

The eagle angrily flew higher and higher, calling out the same question and getting the same answer. At last he was too exhausted to fly any more. He began to glide downward to rest. Then the sparrow let go and flew upwards. The eagle had to admit that the sparrow had won.

45. THE CAT AND THE RAT

The cat and the rat had once bought a firkin of butter together, and hid it under a thick spruce bush.

After that they went a little way off and lay down on a sunny bank to sleep. So when they had lain a while the cat got up, mewed, and bawled out "Yes!"

Then she ran off straight to the firkin and ate a good third part of it. But, when she came back, and the rat asked her where she had been, she said:

"Don't you believe then that I was bidden to a childbed feast."

"So, so," said the rat. "What was the young's name?"

"Just-begun!" said the cat.

So they lay down to sleep again. In a little while up jumped the cat again, bawled out "Yes!" and ran off to the firkin.

This time, too, she ate a good lump. When she came back, and the rat asked her again where she had been, she said:

"Oh! Wasn't I bidden to a naming childbed party again, don't you think?"

"What was the young's name this time?" asked the rat.

"Half-eaten!" said the cat.

The rat thought that a very queer name, but he hadn't wondered long over it before he began to yawn and gape, and fell asleep.

In a little while the cat jumped up as she had done twice before, bawled out "Yes!" and ran off to the firkin, which this time she cleared right out.

When she got back, she told the rat that she had been bidden to a childbed feast again, and when the rat wanted to know the young's name, she answered:

"Licked-to-the-bottom!"

After that they lay down again, and slept a long time; but then they were to go to the firkin to look at the butter, and when they found it eaten up, the rat threw the blame on the cat, and the cat on the rat; and each said the one had been at the firkin while the other slept.

"Well, well," said the cat, "we'll soon find this out, which of us has eaten the butter. We'll just lay down in the sunshine, and he whose cheeks and chin are greasiest when we wake, is the thief."

When the rat lay down, the cat stole off to the firkin for a morsel of butter, which stuck there in a crack. Then